Celestial Echoes

A Collection of Haiku

Brandon Michaels

Celestial Echoes

X

@AuthorBMichaels

Nudous Publishing, LLC

www.nudouspublishing.com

info@nudouspublishing.com

Paperback ISBN: 978-1-964793-95-5

Digital ISBN: 978-1-964793-05-4

Dedication

To the fearless pioneers who dare to defy gravity and venture into the unknown cosmos, "Astral Echoes" is dedicated to you. Your unwavering courage, relentless curiosity, and boundless spirit of exploration have propelled humanity into the far reaches of space and ignited the collective imagination of generations.

This collection of celestial verses is a humble tribute to the astronauts, scientists, engineers, and visionaries who have dedicated their lives to unraveling the mysteries of the universe. Your commitment to pushing the boundaries of space exploration inspires us to dream beyond the stars and fosters a sense of unity that transcends earthly borders.

May these haiku resonate with the echoes of your endeavors, capturing the essence of your extraordinary journeys. As we look to the heavens, we extend our deepest gratitude to those who propel us into the cosmos, boldly paving the way for humanity's odyssey among the stars.

Table of Contents

Part I

Celestial dance,
Astronauts in silver suits,
Moon's gentle embrace.

Starlight whispers soft,
Rocket engines hum a tune,
Galaxies in flight.

Mars, rusty canvas,
Red rover roams the deserts,
Seeking ancient tales.

Orbiting above,
International space home,
Unity in space.

Saturn's rings twirling,
Cassini's final farewell,
Silent cosmic tears.

Jupiter's storms rage,
Galilean moons in ballet,
Astronomy's grace.

Cosmic ballet's end,
Supernovae paint the void,
Stardust is reborn.

Spacewalk ballet, free,
Weightless wonders spin and twirl,
Ethereal dance.

Voyager whispers,
Golden record's message sent,
Humanity's call.

Black hole's mystery,
Einstein's curves in cosmic dance,
Darkness bends the light.

Apollo's first step,
Moon dust beneath the boots' tread,
Human touch in space.

Voyager's journey,
Golden record speaks Earth's tale,
Deep space whispers back.

Hubble's watchful eye,
Galaxies in vibrant hues,
Lost cosmos unveiled.

Pioneer's farewell,
Silent signals to the stars,
Humanity's call.

Sputnik's soft beep-beep,
Echoes in the cosmic void,
Birth of space's song.

Mars rover roams red,
Searching for ancient secrets,
Curiosity.

Shuttle's fiery launch,
Earth to orbit, wings unfurl,
Dreams riding on flames.

Juno's dance with gas,
Jupiter's swirling ballet,
Giant's secrets searched.

The Falcon soars high,
Private hands reach for the stars,
New era takes flight.

I.S.S., a dot,
Floating in orbital grace,
Home for dreams aloft.

Part II

New Horizons' gaze,
Pluto's heart in icy plains,
Distant worlds embraced.

Gaia's cosmic map,
Stars charted in precision,
Universe unfolds.

Stardust in capsule,
Celestial grains in hand,
Time's ancient whispers.

Skylab's silent fall,
Debris becomes shooting stars,
Legacy in flame.

Dragon breathes in space,
Cargo in metallic hold,
Supplies to the stars.

Tiangong orbital,
Chinese whispers in the sky,
Great Wall beyond Earth.

Artemis, rise high,
Lunar gateway beckons near,
Footprints anew traced.

Cygnus in the dark,
Cargo vessel's cosmic arc,
Supplies for the quest.

ExoMars rover,
Red sands beneath its wheels turn,
Martian soil explored.

Osiris-Rex's touch,
Asteroid's regolith found,
Time capsule in stone.

Ariane's ballet,
French Guiana rocket dance,
Payloads in orbit.

Roscosmos launches,
Soyuz in Earth's close embrace,
Russian dreams ascend.

Skylark's grand ascent,
British dreams in the cosmos,
A pioneer's flight.

SpaceShipOne's glide,
XPRIZE victory in the sky,
Commercial space born.

Blue Origin's soar,
New Shepard's suborbital,
Reusable dreams.

Mars helicopter,
Ingenuity takes flight,
An aerial dance.

Soyuz capsule falls,
Cosmonauts return to Earth,
Gravity's embrace.

Starliner's first launch,
Boeing's dreams in the cosmos,
Capsule's journey starts.

Luna's soft light glow,
Russian dreams in the moonlight,
Space race echoes on.

Kepler's watchful eye,
Exoplanets dance in light,
Far beyond our reach.

Part III

Chandrayaan's orbit,
Indian moon mission's gaze,
Craters in the night.

SLS roars to the sky,
Artemis astronauts rise,
Moon's call now answered.

Skylab's orbit fades,
Space station's final farewell,
Legacy in flame.

Gaia's cosmic waltz,
Stellar motions unfolding,
Universe's ballet.

Vostok in the black,
Gagarin's historic flight,
First human in space.

Pioneer's last call,
Silent signals fade away,
Voyager's speaking.

Starliner's return,
Astronauts touch home again,
Earthly reunion.

Starlink's vast array,
Constellations in orbit,
Internet from space.

Soyuz in twilight,
Rockets pierce the evening sky,
Stars watch as we soar.

Viking's Martian gaze,
Red planet's secrets unfold,
A robotic touch.

Skylab's golden age,
Space station in Earth's embrace,
Astronauts in flight.

Atlas V ascent,
Payloads into the unknown,
Rocket's fiery trail.

Hubble's time-travel,
Gazing into ancient light,
Cosmos' memory.

Falcon Heavy roars,
SpaceX power is unleashed
Heavy payloads soar.

Apollo's farewell,
Last footsteps on lunar soil,
Silence in the void.

Cygnus in orbit,
Cargo space delivery,
Supplies for the dream.

Orion's promise,
Deep space dreams in capsule's hold,
Humanity's trip.

Sun's golden embrace,
Planets dance in cosmic waltz,
Solar symphony.

Mercury slow spin,

Swift messenger of the sun,

Fiery fleeting grace.

Venus, morning star,

Shrouded in thick clouds of mist,

Beauty veiled in haze.

Part IV

Earth, cradle of life,
Oceans, forests, deserts thrive,
Blue gem in the void.

Mars, rusty-red orb,
Dusty plains and ancient scars,
Warrior's spirit.

Asteroid belt hums,
Debris between rocky worlds,
Celestial ballet.

Jupiter's grand girth,
Storms rage in striped majesty,
Gas giant's prowess.

Saturn's rings aglow,
Whispers of icy brilliance,
Cosmic jeweled crown.

Uranus tilts, spins,
Pale blue in an azure sea,
A sideways mystique.

Neptune's deep blue hue,
Winds howl in unseen canyons,
Oceanic world.

Pluto, distant heart,
A dwarf among giants shines,
The Kuiper Belt found.

Moons of many tales,
Luna's gentle silver light,
Guardians of night.

Io's fiery rage,
The volcanic fountains spew,
Jupiter's fierce child.

Europa's cold ice,

Subsurface oceans hidden,

Life, hope possible.

Ganymede, largest,

Cratered plains and icy scar,

The Jovian moon.

Callisto, ancient,
Pocked by the countless impacts,
A silent witness.

Titan, Saturn's moon,
Hazy skies, ethereal,
Mysterious world.

Enceladus cries,
Geysers of cold icy plumes,
Erupting secrets.

Triton's retrograde,
Neptune's captured wayward child,
Cold and chaotic.

Phobos and Deimos,
Martian moons in quiet dance,
The red planet's moons.

Charon, Pluto's moon,
Binary partner in cold,
Kuiper Belt duo.

Haumea spins wild,
Dwarf planet in a strange dance,
Elliptical grace.

Makemake, distant,
The Kuiper Belt's icy dwarf,
Far from sun's warm touch.

Part V

Eris, beyond reach,
Dwarf planet in the shadows,
Frozen in the dark.

Interstellar winds,
Voyager's silent journey,
Messages to stars.

Kuiper Belt whispers,
Dwarf planets in cold exile,
Far beyond the sun.

Sunsets on the moon,
Apollo footprints linger,
Cosmic history.

Aurora's ballet,
Magnetic storms in the sky,
Earth's celestial dance.

Hubble's watchful eye,
Peering into deep space realms,
The cosmic wonder.

Cosmic mysteries,
Dark matter's silent presence,
Unseen cosmic force.

Large galactic swirls,
Spirals in vast cosmic seas,
Starbirth and stardeath.

Black holes, gravity,
Consuming all in their path,
Cosmic devourers.

Quasars blaze afar,
Celestial beacons bright light,
Time's relentless march.

Cosmic collisions,
Galaxies in tango dance,
Celestial chaos.

Nebulas unfold,
Stellar nurseries of gas,
Birthplaces of suns.

Space radiation,
Waves from the distant unknown,
Whispering secrets.

Pulsars' rhythmic beats,
Stellar heartbeats in the dark,
Cosmic metronome.

Exoplanet realms,
Far beyond our sun's embrace,
Alien mysteries.

Dark energy's pull,
Expanding universe's song,
Cosmic destiny.

Celestial voyage,
Our solar system's old tale,
Echoes in the void.

Voyager's farewell,
Golden record in the void,
Earth's message to stars.

Liftoff in the blue,
Shuttle soars through cosmic sea,
Earth's embrace below.

Orbiter dances,
Stars applaud in silent night,
Space shuttle ballet.

Part VI

Columbia soars,
Gliding through the edge of space,
Horizon's embrace.

Atlantis in flight,
Cosmic winds whisper secrets,
Shuttle's silent song.

Challenger's ascent,
Hopeful dreams reach for the stars,
Tragedy unfolds.

Discovery sails,
The Orbital symphony,
Notes of weightlessness.

Endeavour's journey,
Bound for the celestial realms,
Destination, space.

Launchpad breathes with fire,
Solid rocket boosters roar,
Shuttle's fiery ascent.

Payload doors open,
Cargo destined for the sky,
Shuttle's cosmic gift.

Hubble in the hold,
Our eyes to the cosmic depths,
Delivered to space.

Astronauts in suits,
Float in microgravity,
Ballet of the brave.

International
Harmony in orbit high,
Unity in space.

Docking with the ISS,
The shuttle's gentle embrace,
Home among the stars.

Spacewalk ballet, free,
Tethered souls in cosmic dance,
Shuttle guards their dreams.

Moonlit rendezvous,
Shuttle meets the lunar orb,
Earth's silent witness.

Payload bay opens,
Satellite set free to soar,
Shuttle's cosmic hand.

The heat shield ablaze,
Reentry through Earth's curtain,
Shuttle's fiery return.

Tiles like armored skin,
Protecting from reentry,
Shuttle's safe descent.

Atlantis' farewell,
Shuttle's final journey ends,
Silent engines rest.

Shuttle in repose,
Museum's gentle cradle,
Echoes of the stars.

Shuttle's roar echoes,
Spacefaring ships flying,
Dreams in rocket trails.

Shuttle's thunder fades,
Orbital echoes linger,
Silence in the void.

Part VII

Shuttle's journey ends,
Beyond the horizon's edge,
Stars whisper goodbye.

Shuttle's final rest,
Celestial voyage complete,
Dreams still in orbit.

Earthbound dreamers gaze,

Sputnik whispers to the stars,

Space age takes its flight.

Gagarin orbits,

Cosmic ballet in the void,

Yuri dances high.

Apollo's footsteps,
Tranquil moonlight on the dust,
Human dreams take flight.

Skylab's sunlit home,
Solar winds and science thrive,
Space station up high.

Shuttle's graceful wings,
Boldly gliding through the dark,
Orbital ballet.

Mir, a Russian star,
Cosmonauts in orbit dance,
Unity in space.

Hubble's lens unveiled,
Galaxies in vivid hues,
Celestial portrait.

Mars rovers explore,
Red planet's ancient secrets,
Curiosity.

International,
Unity in space and time,
Station without bounds.

Tragedy in sky,
Columbia's last descent,
Tears fall for the brave.

Phoenix rising high,
Falcon soars through fiery trails,
Private pioneers.

Rosetta's comet,
Gentle touchdown of Philae,
Cosmic rendezvous.

New Horizons' quest,
Pluto's heart in distant cold,
Frozen mystery.

SpaceX Falcon's dance,
Booster ballet, stage and sky,
Reusable grace.

Starship dreams ascend,
Musk's vision aiming for Mars,
Red frontier awaits.

China's Chang'e rover,
Lunar whispers in the dark,
Jade rabbit's journey.

Gateway to the stars,
Artemis calls to the moon,
Astronauts return.

Tiangong orbit,
China's new celestial home,
Heavenly palace.

Part VIII

Mars Perseverance,
Red dust storm and rover's drive,
Seeking signs of life.

Virgin Galactic,
Branson's joyride to the stars,
Space tourists' delight.

Webb's golden mirror,

Peering into deep expanse,

Universe unveiled.

Gateway to the stars,

Artemis calls to the moon,

Astronauts return.

Kuiper Belt's frontier,
Far beyond Pluto's orbit,
Frozen realms unknown.

Crews capsules journey,
Dragon and Starliner fly,
I.S.S. lifeline.

Gaia's cosmic eye,
Mapping stars in Milky Way,
Stellar census sings.

Space X-rays reveal,
Black holes lurking in the dark,
Gravity's embrace.

Mars Helicopter,
Ingenuity takes flight,
Red skies of conquest.

Quantum entangled,
Communication in space,
Einstein's puzzle solved.

Space debris dances,
Silent waltz of satellite,
Orbits intertwined.

Vostok's echo fades,
Pioneer probes in the void,
Silence of the stars.

Salyut, Skylab, Mir,
Stations in the cosmic sea,
Outposts of mankind.

Dawn on distant worlds,
Planets whispering their tales,
Alien landscapes.

Soyuz' fiery breath,

Earth to orbit and back home,

Soyuz, the lifeline.

Neutron stars collide,

Gravitational waves sing,

Universe in flux.

Spacewalk ballet high,
Tethered to the cosmic stage,
Astronauts float free.

11/14/11

www.ingramcontent.com/pod-product-compliance
Lightning Source LLC
LaVergne TN
LVHW091012080826
845145LV00003B/1242

* 9 7 8 1 9 6 4 7 9 3 9 5 5 *